D0460936

NO LONGER PROPERTY OF
SEATTLE PUBLIC LIBRARY

HALF A GIRAFFE?

JODIE PARACHINI

PICTURES BY
RICHARD SMYTHE

ALBERT WHITMAN & COMPANY
CHICAGO, ILLINOIS

Gisele the giraffe was hungry for leaves,
but the juiciest leaves were at the top of the trees.
She stretched out her neck, but as hard as she tried,
her tongue couldn't reach, so she plopped down and cried.

The zebras and cheetahs and birds gathered 'round
to find what was making that snuffly sound.
And discovered Gisele in a slump by the trees
with her neck in a knot and her chin on her knees.

SNIFF

SNIFF

"Why all the pouting?" the chimpanzee wondered.

"What's all the fuss?" the elephant thundered.

Gisele wiped her tears and gave a small snort,
"What can I do? My neck is too short!"

"I'm just a calf, just a baby giraffe.
When I try to stretch high, the others all laugh.

Why can't I be taller? Just half a neck longer, half a year older, or half a bit stronger?"

"A giraffe and a half? That *would* be a laugh!"
a slow tortoise spoke on the others' behalf.

"Even half a giraffe can be mighty, you'll see,
so rise up and wise up and listen to me—"

"A giraffe is a special and marvelous creature!

Who else has got such a slidable feature?"

"Who else can catch rings on their own set of bumps?
Or high-five the birds without having to jump?"

"What else do you have? Much more than your spots!
Kindness. And pluck. And a headful of thoughts.
You might not have whiskers or armor or wings,
but use what you've got; you don't need those things."

"Stand up and be proud of the body you're given. It's a wonderful place only YOU get to live in!"

A ginormous grin spread as wide as her ears,
as Gisele wiped away all her cold, drippy tears.
She no longer seemed to have legs that were stumpy.
Her knees weren't knobbly. Her spots weren't bumpy!

"I'm half a giraffe," she cried, beaming with pride.
"I can do anything, as long as I've tried."

And setting aside
all her worries and cares,
Gisele climbed
a mountain of...
animal stairs!

And teetering, tottering, she stuck out her tongue,
right to the place where the highest leaf hung.
She grabbed it! And *ate* it! Like she couldn't have done
when she thought of herself as too small and too young.

The lions and hippos all roared with delight,
at witnessing such a spectacular sight.
The meerkats and cheetahs all cheered for Gisele
who wibbled...and wobbled...and oh! Then she...

Down with a *bump* on her small giraffe rump,
but she sat with a grin that her fall couldn't dim.

Dizzy old tortoise just smiled as he shrugged,
and gave her a piece of advice while they hugged:
"You may be small now, and that's okay too,
'cause no matter your size, you will always be you."

For Emmett and his baby brother, Jack,
and for Ana, with love—JP

To my Jurga—RS

Library of Congress Cataloging-in-Publication data is on file with the publisher.

Text copyright © 2018 by Jodie Parachini
Pictures copyright © 2018 by Richard Smythe
First published in the United States of America in 2018 by Albert Whitman & Company
ISBN 978-0-8075-3144-0
All rights reserved. No part of this book may be reproduced or transmitted in any
form or by any means, electronic or mechanical, including photocopying,
recording, or by any information storage and retrieval system,
without permission in writing from the publisher.

Printed in China
10 9 8 7 6 5 4 3 2 1 HH 22 21 20 19 18

Design by Ellen Kokontis

For more information about Albert Whitman & Company,
visit our website at www.albertwhitman.com.